To my daddy

From Kendall and Katelyn

pour mon cher papa

S. B.

I Love My Daddy
Copyright © 2004 Sebastien Braun
Created and produced by Boxer Books Ltd. UK.
Manufactured in China
A hardcover edition of this book was published in the
United Kingdom in 2004 by Boxer Books Limited.
All rights reserved.
www.harperchildrens.com

Library of Congress Cataloging-in-Publication Data

Braun, Sebastien.
I love my daddy / Sebastien Braun — 1st U.S. ed.   p   cm
Summary: A father bear and his cub spend the whole day together.
Reprint. Originally published: U.K. : Boxer Books, 2004
ISBN 0-06-054311-6
[1. Father and child — Fiction.   2. Bears — Fiction.   3. Day — Fiction.] I. Title.
PZ7.B73779Iae 2004   [E]—dc21   2003047860

Typography by Boxer Books Ltd. UK.
6 7 8 9 10

First U.S. edition, 2004

I Love My Daddy

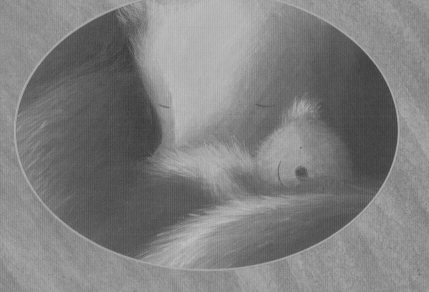

Sebastien Braun

HarperCollinsPublishers

My daddy wakes me.

My daddy feeds me.

My daddy washes me.

My daddy
splashes me.

My daddy plays with me.

My daddy
chases me.

My daddy sits with me.

My daddy
yawns with me.

My daddy
tickles me.

My daddy looks after me.

My daddy cuddles me.

I love my daddy.